A ROCK GROWS UP

THE PACIFIC NORTHWEST
UP CLOSE AND PERSONAL

Written by

Randi Goodrich and Michael Goodrich

Illustrations by

Michele Han

GeoQuest Publications   **Lake Oswego, Oregon**

A ROCK GROWS UP
The Pacific Northwest Up Close and Personal

Goodrich, Randi.
  A rock grows up : the Pacific Northwest up close and personal/
by Randi S. Goodrich and Michael S. Goodrich. -- 1st ed.
  p. cm.
  includes bibliographical references and index.
  ISBN 0-9651101-0-9
  1. Geology--Northwest, Pacific--Juvenile literature. 2. Plate
tectonics--Juvenile literature. 3. Rocks--Juvenile literature.
  I. Goodrich, Michael Scott. II Title.

QE29.G66 1996   **551**
                                QB196-20191

Published by:

GeoQuest Publications
P. O. Box 1665,
Lake Oswego, Oregon 97035

A ROCK IN THE WATER

ISN'T AFRAID OF RAIN

AFRICAN PROVERB

ACKNOWLEDGMENTS

The idea for our book originated in a class taught by Patricia Montgomery and Larry Hanson at Marylhurst College, Marylhurst, Oregon. Initially we researched the book as a labor of love. Then with encouragement and consultation from geologists, elementary teachers, librarians and fourth to sixth grade students, we realized the necessity of telling the earth's story about the rock and plate tectonic cycles.

Warmest thanks to Joan Maiers, Senior Editor, for her careful assessment, and unique sensitivity and love for the written word.

We owe many thanks to our friends for their ongoing encouragement and support. The following are noted for exceptional assistance: Thomas and Tuulikki Abrahamsson, John E. Allen, Sophie Davis, Jen Johnson, Grace Han and Sandra Hoyt.

ABOUT THE AUTHORS

Ever wonder where your favorite rock has traveled? Join Barry Basalt as he shares his personal story with Mike and Randi Goodrich.

Mike Goodrich, B.S., M.S.T., Portland State University, an educator and author for over thirty years, and his wife, Randi, B.A., Marylhurst College, met Barry Basalt on a recent trip to the Oregon Coast.

While carefully preserving scientific content and process, Mike and Randi now share Barry Basalt's story and help demystify complicated rock and plate tectonic theories.

ABOUT THE ILLUSTRATOR

Michele Han, an honor student at Lake Oswego High School in Lake Oswego, Oregon, is a talented local artist, whose illustrations appear in children and adult books. Michele plans to major in elementary education and minor in the visual arts.

DEDICATED TO JEFF

Hardy Quartz

Barry Basalt

Nora Basalt

Sandy Sandstone

CAST

OF

Mary Magnetite

Flo Basalt

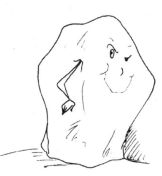

Luke Granite

CHARACTERS

Larry Gneiss

Annie Augite

Michael Mica

Harvey Hornblende

Francis Feldspar

Hi! My name is Barry Basalt (BA-salt). I play an important role in the earth's rock and tectonic (tehk-TAHN-ik) cycle. In the Pacific Northwest, you can find me in lots of places, such as along the scenic Columbia River Gorge or as part of the asphalt paving for Interstate Five. I may even show up as a tiny pebble at the beach.

For a long time I've lived below the earth's crust in the town of Asthenosphere (AS-then-os-fear). Asthenosphere is world-famous for two reasons. First of all, it's extremely hot. Second, the pressure and the temperature achieve a perfect balance so it's a great place for basalts like me to melt!

Last Saturday, I learned that the right time had come to move with my family to the floor of the Pacific Ocean. My sisters, Nora Basalt and Flo Basalt, will find homes of their own. On Monday morning, like toothpaste in a tube, I squeezed through three and three quarter miles (six kilometers) of oceanic crust.

As I oozed out, I grew cooler and cooler. When I arrived at the floor of the Pacific Ocean and my new home in Juan de Fuca (WAN-deh-few-ca), I felt relieved. Later that night, I finally got a chance to look at myself in the mirror. Wow! In just a few hours I had changed from a hot basaltic magma to a cool igneous (IG-nee-us) rock. That means today is my birthday, the day I was born - a heavy, dark and handsome rock!

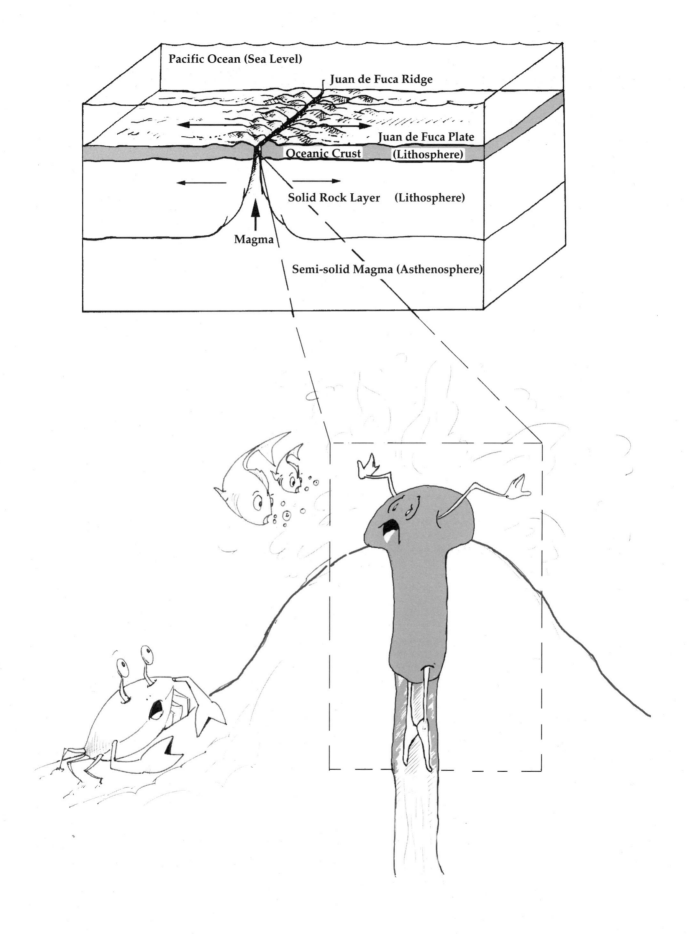

The next day, I decided to visit the Juan de Fuca Amusement Park. I hopped aboard the tectonic roller coaster and settled in for a long trip. My destination was the North American Continental (CON-tin-ental) Plate which is mostly made of granite (GRAN-it). Roller coaster travel is very slow. It is powered by the earth's convection currents, which is just like the movement of boiling water. I traveled about one inch (two to three centimeters) a year. During my trip, sand, silt, clay and the remains of shell organisms (ORGAN-isms) settled on me. After awhile, the ocean materials created a coat of colorful water-soaked sediments, (SED-ih-ments) which I wore for a long time.

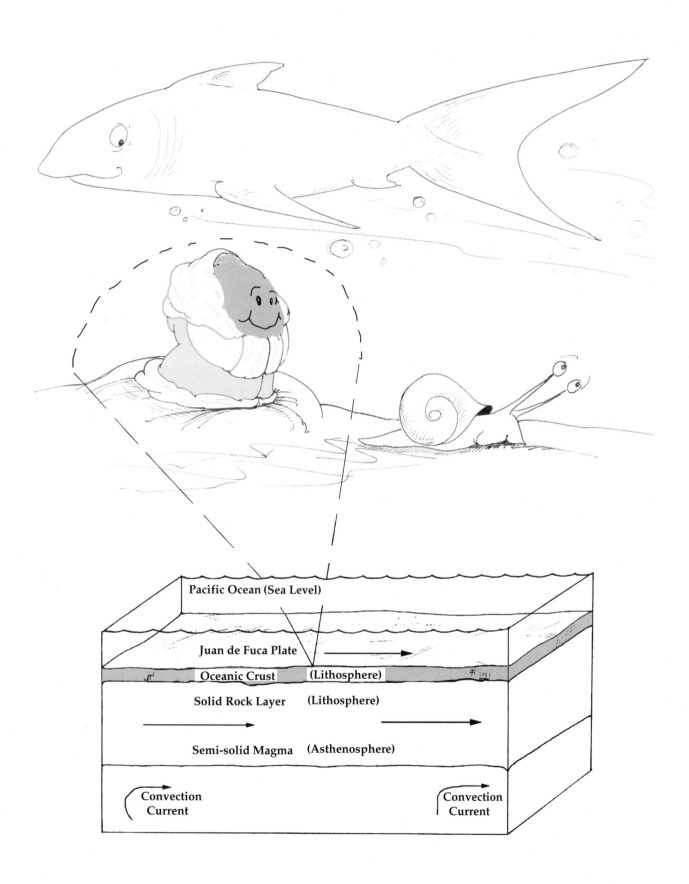

Pacific Ocean (Sea Level)

Juan de Fuca Plate

Oceanic Crust   (Lithosphere)

Solid Rock Layer   (Lithosphere)

Semi-solid Magma   (Asthenosphere)

Convection
Current

Convection
Current

My parents told me the tectonic roller coaster will crash into the massive North American Continental Plate. And when it did, I dove under the plate.

For an hour or so, I explored the town of Crust. Then I took the Crustal bus out to a farm to visit a man who used to live next door to us, Luke Granite. Luke belongs to the family of rocks most frequently found on the Continental Plate. He is a lightweight, multicolored igneous rock. He moved to the Crust area over a thousand years ago.

It was so warm on the bus that when I arrived at Luke's place, I took off my sediment coat. Luke fixed a nice lunch for us, and while we ate, he foretold how after a long time, and with many geologic (GEO-logic) changes, my sediment coat would shape itself into the Coastal Mountains of the Pacific Northwest. After our visit, I said good-by and went on my way again.

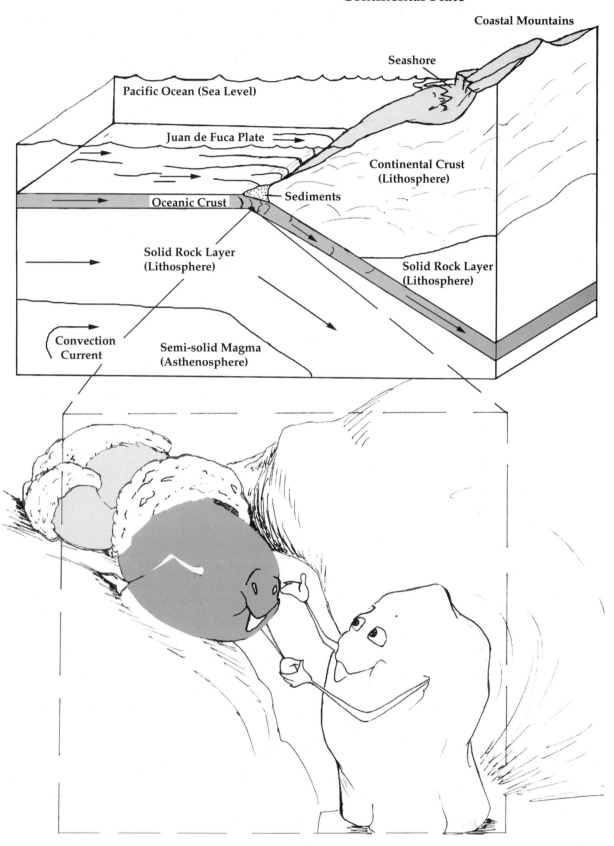

**North American
Continental Plate**

Coastal Mountains

Seashore

Pacific Ocean (Sea Level)

Juan de Fuca Plate

Continental Crust
(Lithosphere)

Oceanic Crust

Sediments

Solid Rock Layer
(Lithosphere)

Solid Rock Layer
(Lithosphere)

Convection
Current

Semi-solid Magma
(Asthenosphere)

Next, I went to see my big sister, Nora Basalt, who lives under the Continental Plate. "Barry," she told me, "I'm feeling a lot of pressure from the North American Continental Plate." She sighed heavily as she said, "I need to move to a new neighborhood, a neighborhood that is closer to the earth's surface. I'd like to settle in the Old Cascades."

"Here, take my magic water ticket," I offered.

"The water will help you melt at a lower temperature. Then you can move away from all the pressure of the Continental Plate."

Nora thanked me warmly and once again I continued on my journey.

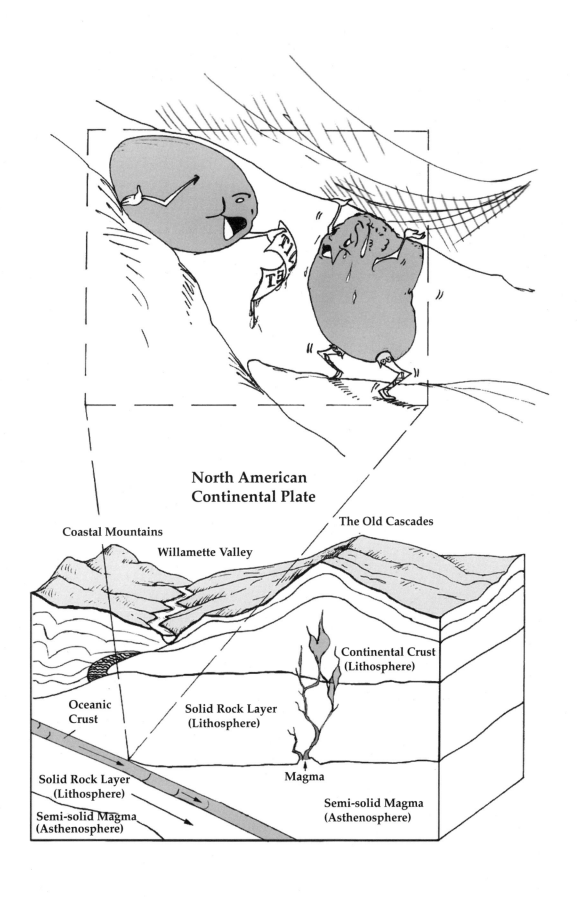

North American
Continental Plate

Coastal Mountains

Willamette Valley

The Old Cascades

Continental Crust
(Lithosphere)

Oceanic
Crust

Solid Rock Layer
(Lithosphere)

Magma

Solid Rock Layer
(Lithosphere)

Semi-solid Magma
(Asthenosphere)

Semi-solid Magma
(Asthenosphere)

With all the excitement of seeing my sister, it occurred to me that I hadn't slept in a long time. I found a cozy place under the Continental Plate and fell fast asleep.

When I awoke, my muscles felt tight. I yawned and stretched to reduce my stiffness.

As I yawned and stretched, I watched the earth begin to move, slowly transmitting seismic (SIZE-mic) waves all around the world. Suddenly I realized that my bending and tilting had created a big tremor within the Continental Plate. I had set off a quake on the earth's surface!

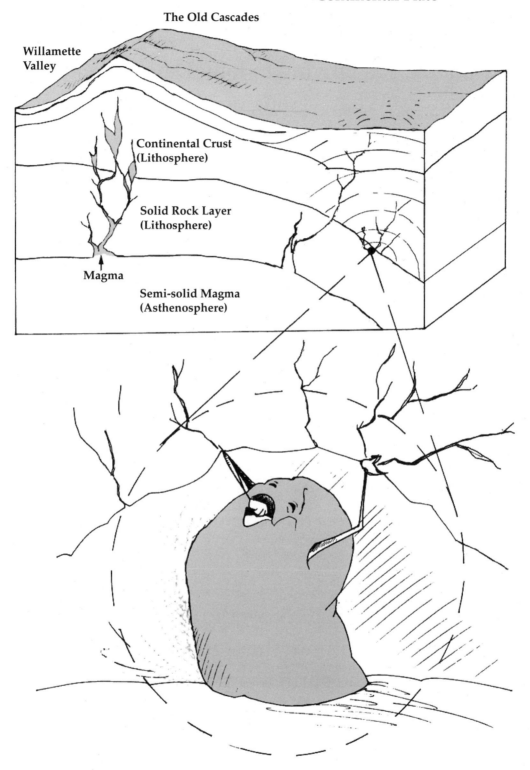

North American
Continental Plate

The Old Cascades

Willamette
Valley

Continental Crust
(Lithosphere)

Solid Rock Layer
(Lithosphere)

Magma

Semi-solid Magma
(Asthenosphere)

The next day, I phoned my little sister, Flo Basalt.

"Barry, I'm moving to John Day, Oregon!"

"What?" "What's going on?" I asked very surprised.

"Well, yesterday, I felt a small tremor, and a few hours later, a great blast of heat filled the entire town. And today my shape is changing!"

"To what?"

"From a semi-solid to a liquid! Finally, I'm ready to move like molasses! "

"That means that the North American Continental Plate has shifted!"

" It also means that now there is enough energy to carry me through eighteen and a half miles (thirty kilometers) of Continental Crust. "

"But, how are you moving up through the earth's crust?"

"Well, I just talked to a friend who lives in John Day. She gave me directions to the earth's thinnest spots. Once I find those fragile places, I can ooze up onto the earth's surface in the form of lava."

"Wow, hot stuff!"

"Well, I've got to go, Barry. You can write me at the Picture Gorge Hotel, John Day, Oregon."

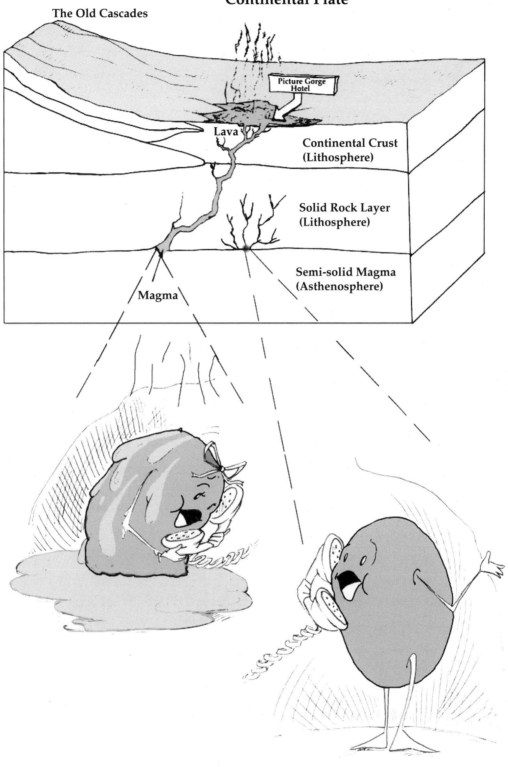

Then it occurred to me! The earth's trembling and shaking would jolt my big sister, Nora, out of her cramped home. So now she could begin a journey of her own.

When I next saw Nora, she introduced me to her new husband, Luke Granite. Luke met my sister when she moved from the Continental Plate to the Old Cascades.

Together Nora and her husband Luke created a new rock family, called Andesite (AN-duh-site). Andesite is a grainy, medium weight rock and looks like sparkling salt and pepper.

Nora and Luke formed an 11,235 foot (3,424 meters) mountain south of Hood River. Long ago, the Native Americans named the mountain Wy'east.Then the British renamed it Mt. Hood, after Samuel Hood, a high-ranking naval officer.

Other famous Northwest andesitic (AN-duh-sit-ic) mountains are Mt. Shasta and Mt. Rainier. My sister and her husband are extremely proud of their mountain. In the summer, they watch climbers from all over America hike Mt. Hood's scenic trails. In the winter, everyone from Olympic teams to local families, enjoys skiing Mt. Hood's beautiful slopes.

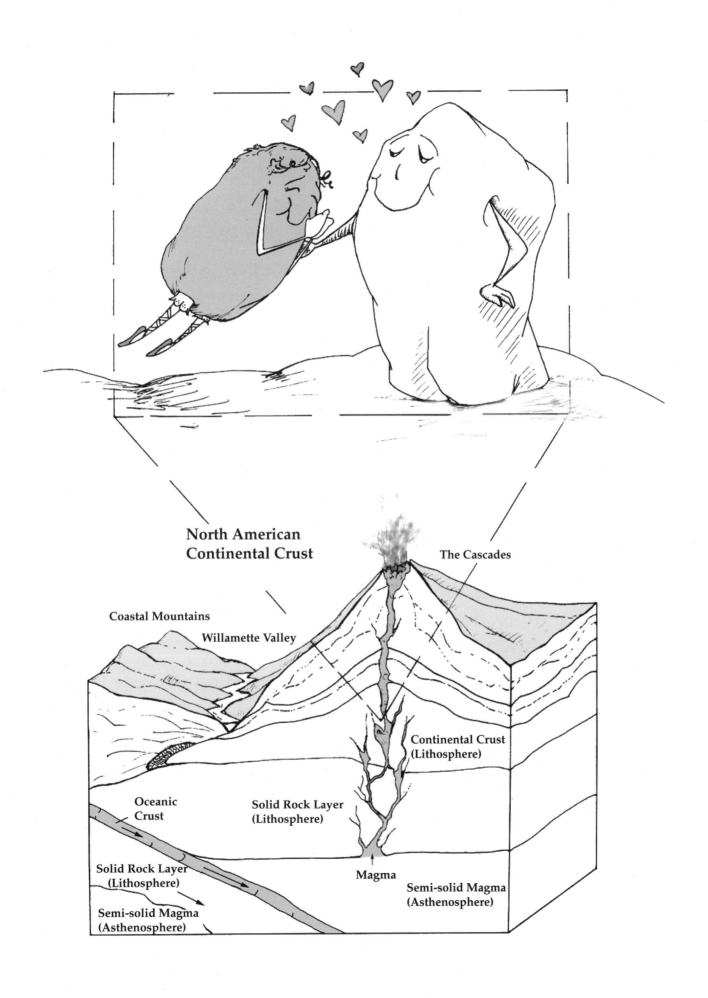

North American
Continental Crust

The Cascades

Coastal Mountains

Willamette Valley

Continental Crust
(Lithosphere)

Oceanic
Crust

Solid Rock Layer
(Lithosphere)

Solid Rock Layer
(Lithosphere)

Magma

Semi-solid Magma
(Asthenosphere)

Semi-solid Magma
(Asthenosphere)

My sister, Nora, and her husband produced a family of four mineral children. The children's names are: Michael Mica (MY-cah), Francis Feldspar (FELD-spar), Annie Augite (Ah-jite), and Harvey Hornblende (HORN-blend). They spent many years living together as part of Mt. Hood.

One day I phoned my sister.

Sounding very tired, she said, "Barry, life as a mountain is so difficult. The intense heat of the summer sun causes us to expand. The cold icy snows of winter forces us to contract. Then the harsh winds and the pounding rains tear away at our soft, top layers. Year after year, the constant attack of the rains decomposes or chemically weathers us. The extreme temperatures, the harsh winds and the abrasive stream activity fragment or break down the sides of our mountain."

"This process of fragmentation is called physical weathering. We've been here a long, long time. The sun, together with the ice, wind and rain, has worn us down. But, Barry, it's the ice, or the glacial erosion, that has affected us most of all."

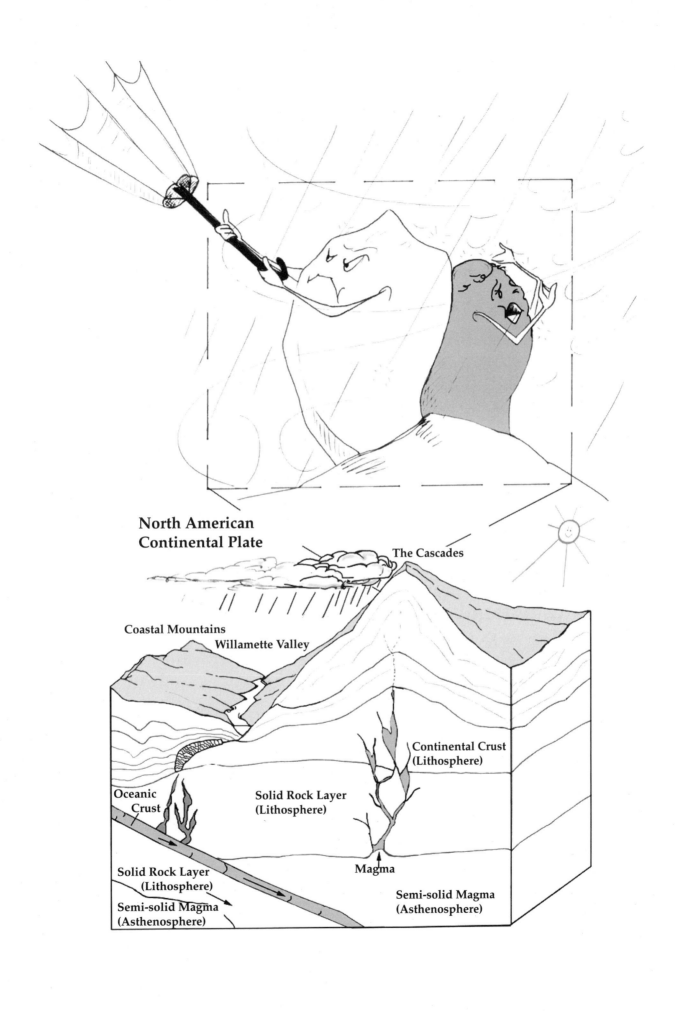

North American
Continental Plate

The Cascades

Coastal Mountains

Willamette Valley

Continental Crust
(Lithosphere)

Oceanic
Crust

Solid Rock Layer
(Lithosphere)

Magma

Solid Rock Layer
(Lithosphere)

Semi-solid Magma
(Asthenosphere)

Semi-solid Magma
(Asthenosphere)

The weathering process was especially hard on Michael Mica and Francis Feldspar. In May, they broke into tiny chunks. In August, they rolled down the mountainside and into the river.

"Where are they now?" I asked.

"The sticky Clay family adopted them. The children called last week to say they are quite happy living in the Willamette Valley."

"That's great."
I was curious about my other two relatives.

"Where are Annie Augite and Harvey Hornblende?" I asked.

"Well, as heavier minerals they are more resistant to the weathering process. So they will weather more slowly. At just the right time, they will move away from home. Then they too will be adopted by the sticky Clay family and live along the muddy banks of the Willamette River. It's all part of our rock life cycle."

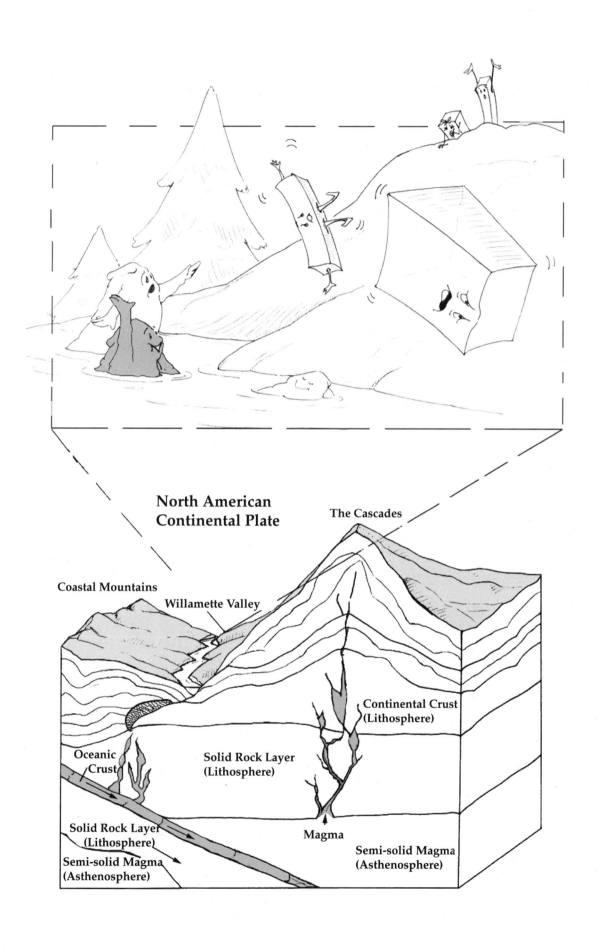

North American Continental Plate

The Cascades

Coastal Mountains

Willamette Valley

Continental Crust (Lithosphere)

Oceanic Crust

Solid Rock Layer (Lithosphere)

Magma

Solid Rock Layer (Lithosphere)

Semi-solid Magma (Asthenosphere)

Semi-solid Magma (Asthenosphere)

I asked my sister, "will they live with the sticky Clay family forever?"

"No. Living with the sticky Clay family prepares the children for the next step in the rock cycle. This is an in-between stage, a time of adjustment. It's one of many stops along the way as the children prepare to become a new kind of rock."

"So they live along the river bank for awhile and then what happens?"

"Each day, as the river flows down the mountain side it brings with it new materials which are deposited along the river banks. These materials will also become part of the sticky Clay family. When the new members move in with the sticky Clay family they put a lot of pressure on the old family members. This pressure buries the old family members and pushes them into the earth, where they are cemented together. After they bond, they become the Shale (SHH-ale) family, a layered, sedimentary (SED-ih-men-tree) rock. Then with more pressure from all the newly deposited material, and a little heat from within the earth, metamorphic (Met-a-MORE-fick) rock families emerge, such as Slate (SL-ate), Schist (SHH-ist), and Gneiss (NICE)."

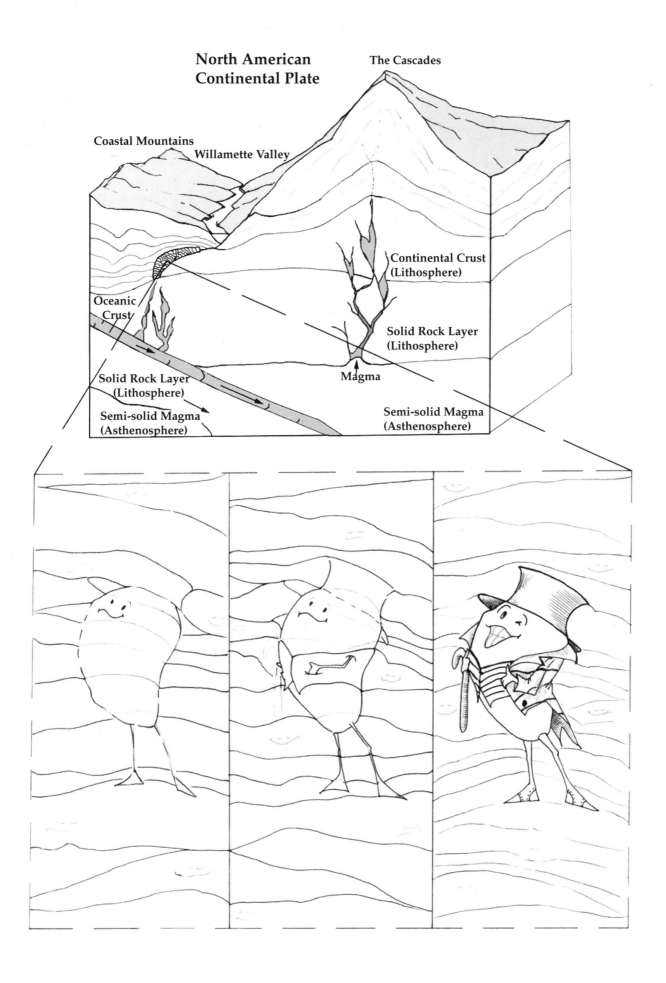

She continued, "This is the process that created Larry Gneiss."

"I remember him! I met him a long time ago. And when I was very little I always asked you why he dressed as though he was off to a fancy party."

"Yes." And she explained that Larry dressed that way because he knew that if he traveled too close to a magma pool, he would turn into a magma. Then he could never wear his fancy black and white suit again.

The last time I saw Larry Gneiss, he was thousands of years old. He told me many stories about how the weathering process had ruined his handsome black and white look.

Years later I learned that Larry Gneiss had crumbled.

Happily, however, this process enabled his daughter, Mary Magnetite, (MAAG-ni-tite) to travel to the beach.

One day I received a letter from Mary Magnetite. She wrote to tell me that she met her mineral friend Hardy Quartz (KWORTS) at the beach. Recently, they decided to join other minerals, rocks and shells to form sand.

Mary Magnetite wrote, "Oh Barry, it's such great fun to be sand! Sand is stroked, patted and caressed by wonderful big and little people who build castles by the sea!"

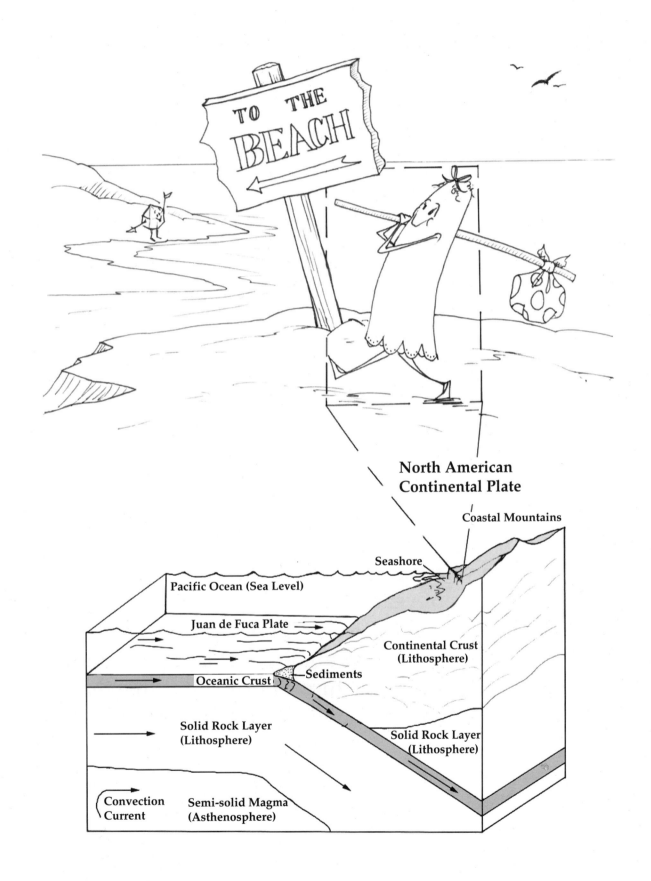

**North American
Continental Plate**

Coastal Mountains

Seashore

Pacific Ocean (Sea Level)

Juan de Fuca Plate

Continental Crust
(Lithosphere)

Oceanic Crust

Sediments

Solid Rock Layer
(Lithosphere)

Solid Rock Layer
(Lithosphere)

Convection
Current

Semi-solid Magma
(Asthenosphere)

TO THE BEACH

I remember when I lived at the beach. I loved the blowing winds and the rise and the fall of the tides as they moved the sand out to the sea, then back to the beach and then out to the sea again. I remember how the sand was sorted by size and weight. I watched how the rhythmical motion of the waves softened their characters. I remember how the sediments were pressed together to form layers under the ocean.

Over a very long period of time, water and chemicals seeped through the sediment layers and cemented the grains together. I remember how one layer on top of another was built from the sediments. I remember my next door neighbor, Sandy Sandstone (SAND-stone). He was created in just this way.

Sandy Sandstone was mostly made of quartz (KWORTS). He was lightweight and variously colored from years of exposure to dripping water. Over thousands of years, the heavy sediments which were deposited offshore forced him deeper and deeper into the earth. Eventually, heat and pressure changed his shape and texture. Shortly after that, he joined the metamorphic family.

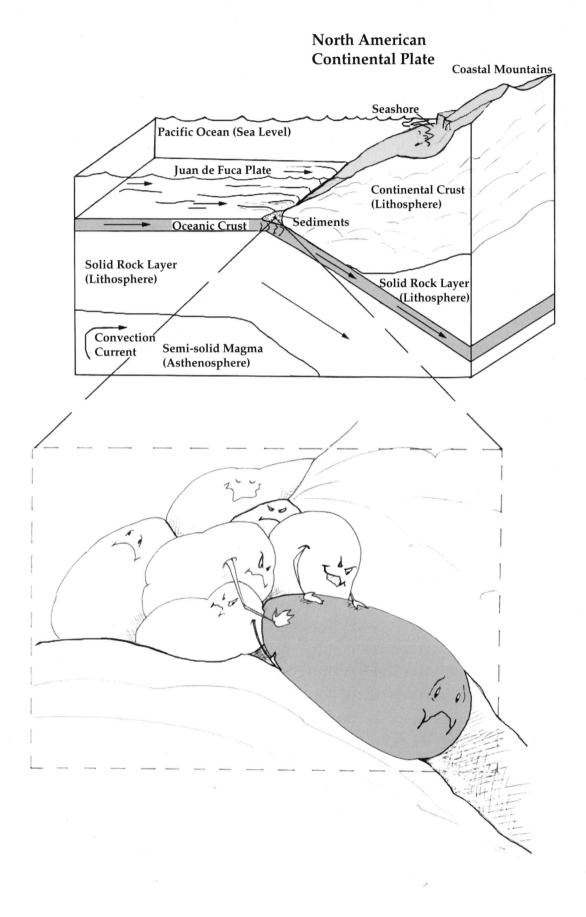

As you can see from my story every rock's life is unique. The life cycle of every rock follows its own natural rhythm. Every rock undergoes a transitional process: first a formless life, then a lifestyle of finding form and structure, and then returning to formlessness. And so it is with me. One day I found myself back on the tectonic roller coaster, settling in for a long journey. After thousands of years and millions of miles, I'm ready to return home to Juan de Fuca. I figure I'll arrive there just in time for my birthday!

TURN THE PAGE NOW

TO REVISIT BARRY'S

FAMILY AND FRIENDS

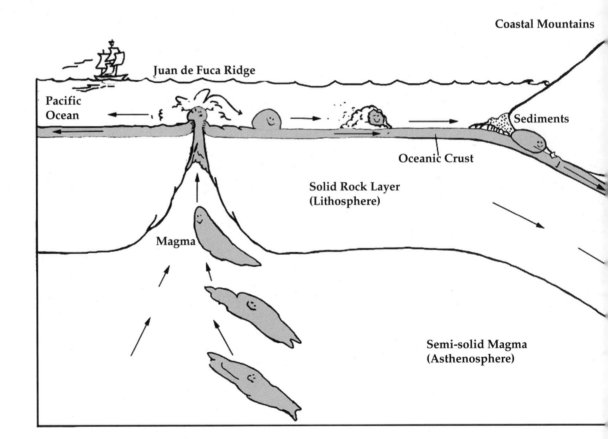

Coastal Mountains

Juan de Fuca Ridge

Pacific
Ocean

Sediments

Oceanic Crust

Solid Rock Layer
(Lithosphere)

Magma

Semi-solid Magma
(Asthenosphere)

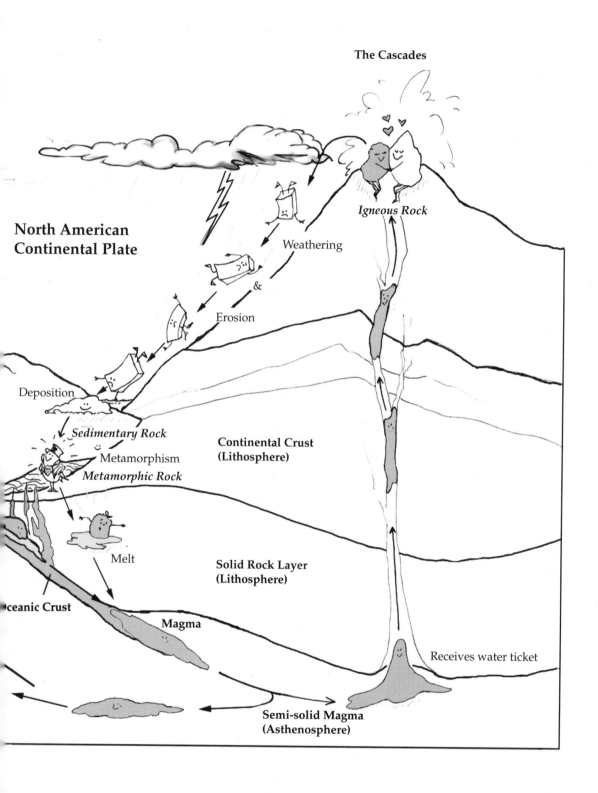

The Cascades

Igneous Rock

**North American
Continental Plate**

Weathering

&

Erosion

Deposition

Sedimentary Rock

Metamorphism

Metamorphic Rock

**Continental Crust
(Lithosphere)**

Melt

**Solid Rock Layer
(Lithosphere)**

Oceanic Crust

Magma

Receives water ticket

**Semi-solid Magma
(Asthenosphere)**

Works Cited

Dictionary of Geological Terms. Rev. ed (1962) Garden City: Dolphin Books,
   1962.

Allen, John Eliot. **The Magnificent gateway; a layman's guide to the geology of
   the Columbia River Gorge.** Portland: Timber Press, 1979.

Erickson, Jon. **Plate Tectonics: Unraveling The Mysteries of the Earth.**
    New York: Facts on File, Inc., 1992.

Harris, Stephen L. **Fire Mountains of the West: The Cascades and Mono Lake
   Volcanoes.** Missoula: Mountain Press Publishing Co., 1988.

Klein, Cornelis, and Cornelius S. Hurlbut, Jr. **Manual of Mineralogy** (after
   James D.Dana). 21st ed. New York: John Wiley & Sons, Inc., 1993.

Mottana, Annibale, Rodolfo Crespi, and Giuseppe Liborio. **Simon & Schuster's
   Guide to Rocks & Minerals.** Trans. Catherine Athill, Hugh Young and
   Simon Pleasance. New York: Simon & Schuster, 1978.

Orr, Elizabeth L., and William N. Orr. **Geology of the Pacific Northwest.**
   New York: McGraw-Hill Companies, Inc., 1996

Orr, Elizabeth L., William N. Orr, and Ewart M. Baldwin. **Geology of Oregon.**
   4th ed. Dubuque: Kendall/Hunt Publishing Company, 1992.

Plummer, Charles C., and David McGeary. **Physical Geology.** 6th ed.
   Dubuque: W.C. Brown Publishers, 1993.

Scarth, Alwyn. **Volcanoes.** College Station: Texas A & M University Press,1994.

Works Cited

Wood, Charles A., and Jurgen Kienle. eds. **Volcanoes of North America:**

    United States and Canada. Cambridge: Cambridge University Press,

    1991.

Zoehfeld, Kathleen Weidner. **How Mountains Are Made.** New York:

    Harper Collins, 1995.

Glossary

Andesite   (AN-duh-site) A fine-grained gray and white speckled rock found in lavas of the Cascade Mountains.

Augite   (AH-jite) A dark green to black mineral found in igneous rocks like andesite and basalt.

Basalt   (BA-salt) A fine-grained dark gray to black igneous rock commonly found in lavas of the Pacific Northwest.

Asthenosphere

     (AS-then-os-fear) The semi-solid magma region of the earth which is located beneath the lithosphere.

Continental Plate   (CON-tin-ental) Large granite slabs located in the Earth's rigid outer shell. These slabs or plates are in constant motion. This motion creates earthquake and volcanic activity.

Convection Current | (KAN-vek-shen) The movement of material due to differences in density brought about by heating.

Feldspar | (FELD-spar) A group of light-colored minerals, usually pink, gray or white, that are commonly found in rocks.

Geology | (JE-all-o-je) The study of the earth's surface and its interior.

Gneiss | (NICE) A banded or striped coarse-grained metamorphic rock that formed deep under the ground. Found in the Siskiyou, Blue and Wallowa Mountains of Oregon and the North Cascades of Washington.

Granite | (GRAN-it) A light-colored, coarse-grained, igneous rock found in the Siskiyou, Blue and Wallowa Mountains.

Hornblende | (HORN-blend) A shiny black mineral most commonly found in igneous and metamorphic rocks.

Igneous Rock	(IG-nee-us) (From the Latin word which means fire.) Igneous rock is formed when hot magma or lava cool and harden. Basalt, granite and andesite are examples of igneous rocks.
Juan de Fuca	(WAN-deh-few-ca) One of several oceanic plates located off the Northwest coast of North America.
Lava	(LAH-va) Magma that flows out of the earth and onto its surface.
Lithosphere	(LITH-os-fear) (Litho- from the Greek word which means rock.) The solid outer layer of the earth.
Magnetite	(MAAG-ni-tite) A black, heavy magnetic mineral often found in beach sands of the Pacific Northwest. Also commonly found in dark igneous rocks.
Magma	(MAAG-ma) Liquid rock inside the earth.

Metamorphic	(Met-a-MORE-fick) (From the Greek word which means to change form.) Igneous or sedimentary rock that is changed by heat and pressure underground. Often found in mountain ranges in the Pacific Northwest. Gneiss, marble and schist are examples of metamorphic rocks.
Mica	(MY-cah) A group of minerals that are black, clear, or gold-colored. Found in igneous, sedimentary or metamorphic rocks. Mica splits easily into thin sheets.
Mineral	(MIN-er-al) A non-living crystalline solid with a definite composition found in nature. Quartz, magnetite, mica, feldspar, augite, and hornblende are examples of minerals.

Oceanic Crust	(o-SHE-an-ic) Large basalt slabs located in the earth's rigid outer shell. These slabs or plates are in constant motion. This motion creates earthquake and volcanic activity.
Plate Tectonics	(Tehk-TAHN-iks) An important geologic theory stating that the Earth's hard outer shell is broken up into about thirteen large slabs or plates that float on the asthenosphere.
Quartz	(KWORTS) A multi-colored (white, black, green, blue, red or clear) mineral commonly found in rocks.
Rock	A material composed of one or more minerals.
Rock Cycle	A process which involves heat, pressure, melting, cooling and sedimentation, whereby rocks change from one type to another.

Sandstone   (SAND-stone) A sedimentary rock that was formed when quartz sediments were cemented together and pressure was applied until it hardened. The coast ranges of Oregon and Washington and inland lakes and streams often contain sandstones.

Schist   (SHH-ist) A medium to coarse grained metamorphic rock.

Sediment   (SED-ih-ment) (From the Latin word which means settled.) Loose, solid particles which come from the weathering and erosion of rocks.

Sedimentary Rock   (SED-ih-men-tree) Pieces of clay, mud, sand and organic materials which have been hardened by cement and pressure. Sandstone, shale, coal and conglomerates are examples of sedimentary rock.

Shale   (SHH-ale) A layered, sedimentary rock of pressed clay or mud.

Slate   (SL-ate) A fine grained, metamorphic rock associated with low pressure and temperature.

Weathering   (WETH-ur-ing) The effects of air, wind, ice, heat, water, and rain on solid rock which forces the rock to break down into smaller particles called sediments.

INDEX

Andesite 24
Augite 26
Asthenosphere 10

Basalt 10

Continental Plate 14
Convection Current 14

Feldspar 26

Geology 45
Gneiss 30
Granite 14

Hornblende 26

Igneous 12

Juan de Fuca 12

Lava 22
Lithosphere 46

Magnetite 34
Magma 12
Metamorphic 30
Mica 26
Mineral 47

Oceanic Crust 48

Plate Tectonics 48

Quartz 34

Rock 48
Rock Cycle 48

Sandstone 36
Schist 30
Sedimentary 30
Shale 30
Slate 30

Weathering 26

More from GeoQuest Publications

A Rock Grows Up: A Curriculum Guide $7.95
Randi Goodrich and Michael Goodrich

This guide is for people who want to know more about Northwest
Geology. It provides the teacher with well organized information
for student participation in: lab exercises, coloring activities and creative
writing. Further, the guide offers supportive resources such as visuals;
computer programs; guest speakers; internet locations; field trips and
science equipment. Hand collected rock and mineral proverbs provide
the students with ageless wisdom.

Rock and Mineral Kit $14.95
Randi Goodrich and Michael Goodrich

Twelve tagged samples of the rocks and minerals mentioned in
A Rock Grows Up provides students with hands on experience.
Through investigation the students learn to identify the characteristics
and properties of rocks and minerals. The samples may be used in
conjunction with the story, the curriculum guide or for independent
classroom activities.

ORDER FORM

✳ Fax Orders   (503) 635-4420 (Available to schools and libraries)

☎ Telephone Orders   (503) 635-4420 (Available to schools and libraries)
🖃 Postal Orders   GeoQuest Publishing, M.R. Goodrich,
                               P. O. Box 1665 Lake Oswego, OR. 97035, USA.
                               Tel: (503) 635-4420
                               Please enclose your check or money order

Business or School Name _____

School's Purchase Order Number _____

Name _____

Address _____

City_____State_____Zip_____-_____

Telephone (____)_____

Contact GeoQuest Publications for multiple order discounts.

Please send ____copy/copies of the book @ $9.95 ea. $ _____

Please send ____box/boxes of rocks & minerals @ $14.95 ea.   _____

Please send ____copy/copies of the Curriculum Guide @ $7.95   _____

I understand that I may return the book or curriculum guide for a full refund for any reason. No questions asked.

Shipping and Handling :

         Book rate: $2.50 for each book   _____
         Curriculum Guide: $2.50 each guide   _____

         (Surface shipping may take 3-4 weeks)

         Priority: $ 3.50 per book   _____
                   $ 3.50 per curriculum guide   _____

         Rocks and Minerals Box: $4.50 per box   _____

Payment:

Check for $ _____ enclosed   **TOTAL** $_____